Delilah Darling
is in the Classroom

For Elizabeth Morris – J.W.

Best wishes, Goldy – R.R.

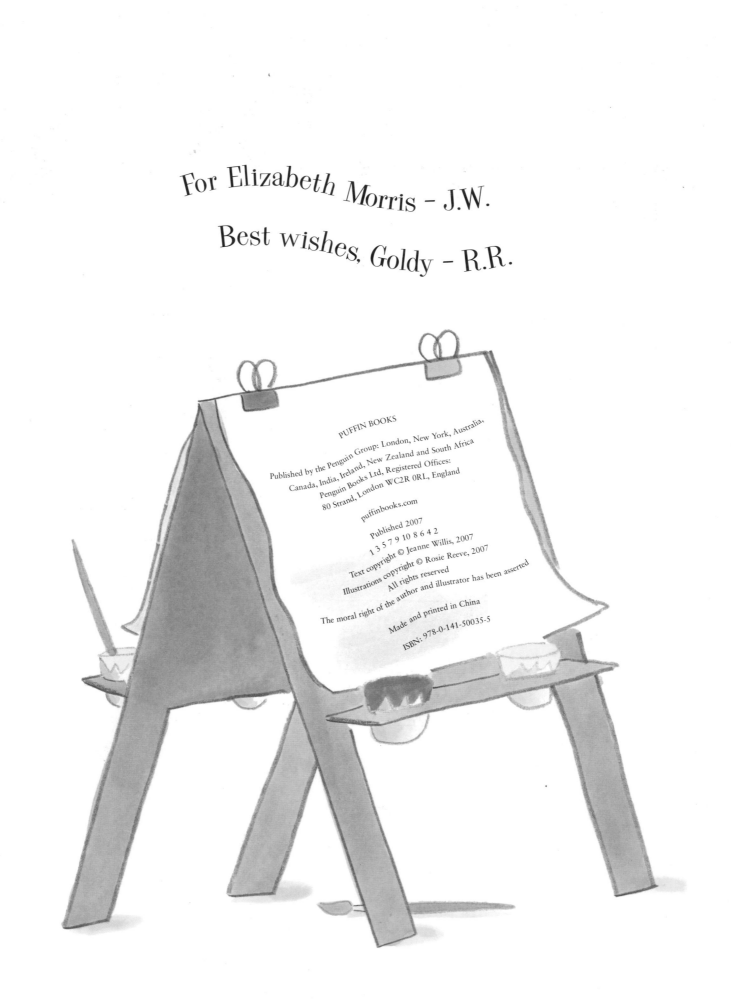

PUFFIN BOOKS

Published by the Penguin Group: London, New York, Australia,
Canada, India, Ireland, New Zealand and South Africa
Penguin Books Ltd, Registered Offices:
80 Strand, London WC2R 0RL, England

puffinbooks.com

Published 2007

1 3 5 7 9 10 8 6 4 2

Text copyright © Jeanne Willis, 2007
Illustrations copyright © Rosie Reeve, 2007
All rights reserved

The moral right of the author and illustrator has been asserted

Made and printed in China

ISBN: 978-0-141-50035-5

Delilah Darling

is in the Classroom

Jeanne Willis

Illustrated by Rosie Reeve

My name is Queen Delilah.
I come from a land far, far away.

Really I do.

But my mother says,

"**Really**, you don't, darling. You come from **here** and so does your little brother."

That is **nonsense**, I'm afraid.
She's even **forgotten** I'm a **queen**,
otherwise she'd let me have
a pet **rhinoceroo**.

Where I really come from, all the best queens have at least eleventy rhinoceroos.

But my mother says,
"Delilah, **darling**,
you're making it all up.
Besides, you already have
a cat **and** a dog."

Well, maybe not all queens
have **eleventy** rhinoceroos,
but they all have **some**
and I'm not allowed **any**.

It's NOT fair!

It's snowing today.
I want to wear my sparkly heels,
but my mother says,

"Delilah, darling, you are not wearing
those to school!"

So I say, "Why not?
Where I come from, everyone wears
sparkly heels in the snow."

I'm not allowed to wear my golden crown either.
So I've made one out of paper.

It's in my lunch box
under my cheese sandwich.

Here I am walking to school with Gigi.
Gigi is my Old Pear.
She came from a town called France to
look after me and my brother, Smallboy,
but really I'm the one who
looks after her.

WHEATFIELDS INFANTS

See? I have to hold her hand so
she doesn't run into the road.

In the cloakroom, Mrs Mullet says,
"Pick your coat up and **hang** it on your peg."

What a funny place to put it! Where I come from,
we all

hang

our

coats

on

the

floor.

This is me in school **assembly**
with my **best** boyfriend,
Lucian Lovejoy.

Assembly is when you have to sit on the floor
and listen to bla bla bla until your bum goes numb.

In assembly where I come from,
we're allowed to bring big pets like
rhinoceroos, girooffs
and gorilloes
to sit on.
They're very
comfortable actually.

"What if you only have a small pet,
like a newt?" whispers Lucian.
"Then they are allowed
to sit on us," I tell him.

"Lucian Lovejoy, stop giggling!"
shushes Mrs Mullet.
I don't know why.
Where I come from, it's rude
not to giggle if it's funny.

Now I'm doing sums.
Mrs Mullet says,
"What does one cake plus another cake make?"
And I say, "I know, I know!
It makes you sick!"

Mrs Mullet says,
"Delilah Darling, please don't shout out
and, Lucian Lovejoy, stop laughing!
What is one plus one?"

He doesn't know so I whisper the answer in his ear.

"It's eleventy!"
he says.

"There is no such number as eleventy," says Mrs Mullet.

But there is where I come from!
We count like this:

One-ga, toodle, threeba, fourbo, fiva, sixbi, sevenba, eightish, ninsy, tenga . . . eleventy!

After sums, we do P.E.

P.E. is short for **Prancing Excitedly**.

At least it is in the land where I come from.

But Mrs Mullet says to choose a partner

and pretend to be **mice**.

So me and Lucian go

crash,

crash,

thump.

And

Rarggg

gggh!

Mrs Mullet shouts, "What are you doing?
Mice are tiny, quiet creatures!"
And Lucian says, "Not where Delilah comes from!"

"Yes!" I say. "In the land where I come from, the mice are huge and noisy. They go BLAM! BLAM! BLAM!

"BLAM!"

"Not in my class, they don't!"
  says Mrs Mullet. "Be sleeping mice!"
So we go,
  "SNORE!
    SNORE!
      SNORE!"

"There are days," says Mrs Mullet,
  "when I wish I worked in a library."

Mrs Mullet says she is so glad it's **Playtime**. It's my favourite too!

I've got my skipping rope. Horrid Charlotte Griggs says, "I bet YOU can't skip to ten."

So

I count

1 one-ga, 2 toodle, 3 threeba, 4 fourb-

...**OW!**

"Ha, ha!" laughs
Horrid Charlotte.

But where I come from, we **always** fall over
when we get to **fourbo** – it's the rules.
I bet **she** can't do it.

Charlotte says, "Bet I can!"
and falls over brilliantly.

Now **everyone** wants to try.

"Stop that game!" says Mrs Mullet.
"The school nurse will run out of plasters."

After Playtime, we do Art.
Today, whoever **paints** the best **animal picture** gets to
keep Polly and Dolly, the school hamsters, for the weekend.

Lucian can't think of any animals,
so I tell him to paint a hamster.

Here's my picture of the pets that live
in my Far Away Palace.

"Look at Delilah's **wonderful** painting of **guinea pigs!**" says Mrs Mullet.

But anyone can see they're **not** guinea pigs! **They're rhinoceroos!**

I wonder if Mrs Mullet needs glasses.

Yippee!

I've been chosen to look after Polly and Dolly.

Only Polly is covered in blue spots.

"I hope she's not ill," says Mrs Mullet.

"It's all right," says Lucian. "Delilah Darling told me to paint a hamster, so I did."

When Gigi picks me up from school
she says my painting is *magnifique*.
She can tell it's a herd of
rhinoceroos straight away.
They know a lot about art,
the French.

The next day, Gigi says, "*Ooh la la!*
I thought there were two hamsters?"
"Yes — Polly and Dolly," I tell her.

But Gigi says,
"I think you are not learning
your sums, Delilah. Count again!"